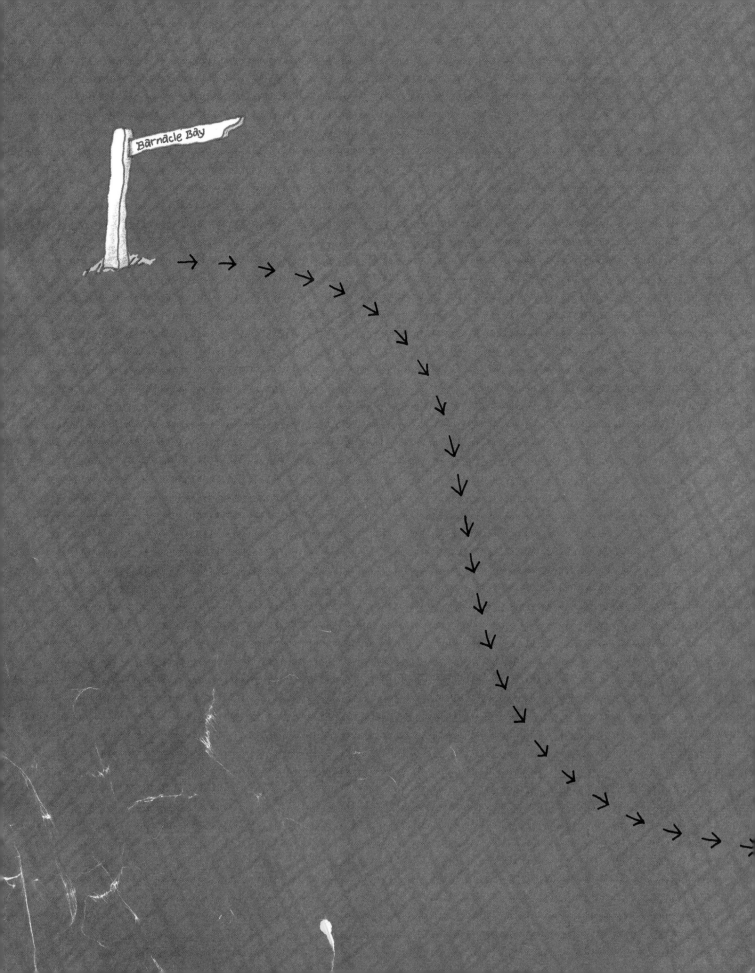

PIRATE TREASURE MAP

A Fairytale Adventure

For Molly . . . a treasure!

Copyright © 2006 by Colin and Jacqui Hawkins

First published in 2006 by Walker Books Ltd.
87 Vauxhall Walk, London SE11 5HJ

First U.S. edition 2007

Library of Congress Cataloging-in-Publication Data is available.

Library of Congress Catalog Card Number 2006042570

ISBN-13: 978-0-7636-3205-2
ISBN-10: 0-7636-3205-8

10 9 8 7 6 5 4 3 2 1

Printed in China

This book has been typeset in Cochin.
The illustrations were done in watercolor and color pencil.

Candlewick Press
2067 Massachusetts Avenue
Cambridge, Massachusetts 02140

visit us at www.candlewick.com

PIRATE TREASURE MAP

A Fairytale Adventure

Colin & Jacqui Hawkins

CANDLEWICK PRESS
CAMBRIDGE, MASSACHUSETTS

Mrs. Hubbard

Jack Hubbard

Patch

Once upon a time, Jack Hubbard, his mom, Old Mother Hubbard, and their dog, Patch, all lived together at The Dish and Spoon Inn, a small tavern on the busy harbor of Barnacle Bay.

"I always wanted to have my own little place by the sea," said Mother Hubbard, "and all those gold sovereigns from the Giant really came in handy."

Jack was pleased that his mom was happy, but he longed for adventure.

Then, one dark and stormy night, the tavern door crashed open and in strode . . .

Cap'n Horatio Hubbard.

He was Jack's long-lost uncle, who had set out many years
before on his adventures across the seven seas aboard
the good ship *Goosey Gander*.

That night,

as Cap'n Hubbard chowed down on his favorite grub of mac and cheese and

swigged down tankards of dandelion and burdock, he told tall tales of hairy-scary adventures on the high seas, of witches, trolls, magic, and enchanted lands. Jack's eyes widened as his uncle spoke of a faraway island where a fabulous treasure lay hidden deep within the crumbling walls of an ancient tower.

"No one will ever find their way to this treasure without a very old and forgotten map. But, look, me hearties, 'ere it be!" And with a flourish, out from under his hat, Cap'n Hubbard produced a tattered parchment. "This be old Bony Rattle's map, and on the morning tide we sails to find the treasure. And we needs a cabin boy. So why don't ye join us, Jack?

Waddya say?"

Jack didn't need to be asked twice. Early the next morning he kissed his mom good-bye.

Full of excitement,

Jack and Patch clambered aboard the *Goosey Gander*. They set sail in fine weather, heading west. Then they steered northwest through the dangerous realm of the sea serpents. Jack soon had a taste for this adventurous life on the high seas.

Shake a leg, landlubbers!

However, he was not so sure about some of the crew, who looked rather hairy, shifty, and sly—especially Wicked Ed Wolf, the first mate, a fearsome-looking character with an eye patch and a peg leg.

Jack's unease was confirmed when, late at night, through an open hatch, he heard furtive mumbling from below deck. He crept to the edge and peered down. There, huddled together, deep in muttered conversation, were Wicked Ed Wolf and his treacherous cronies.

"So, 'tis agreed," grunted Wicked Ed, "at noon tomorrow we takes the ship. Then we takes the treasure map, and then we throws Cap'n Hubbard overboard and any other lubber who ain't wiv us. Aye! Then we finds the treasure! And then we is rich! Ha-har!"

Jack crept away. He had to warn Cap'n Hubbard. . . .

The next day, as they were heading north around the Ragged Rocks, a great storm began to rage. The wind howled, and huge waves battered the ship from side to side.

"'Tis a fearsome storm when the north wind blows, Jack!" yelled Cap'n Hubbard as he grappled with the ship's wheel. At that very moment, Wicked Ed Wolf and his mutinous gang appeared.

"Aye, Cap'n, 'tis an ill wind! Ha-har!" snarled Wicked Ed, pointing his pistol at Cap'n Hubbard. "I'm takin' the *Goosey,* and I'll 'ave yer 'at and the treasure map that be 'idden inside it. Wassit to be, Cap'n? Yer 'at or yer 'ead? Haw, haw!"

"Neither, you hairy scoundrel! I'm ready for your evil game," roared Cap'n Hubbard, and he let go of the ship's wheel. The *Goosey Gander* rolled hard to one side, sending huge waves crashing over the ship. Wicked Ed lost his balance and hit the deck!

Then . . . *BOOM!*

Wicked Ed's pistol fired and blew Cap'n Hubbard's hat clean off his head and into the wild sea below.

"Lummy! Me hat!" shouted Cap'n Hubbard.

"Aaaargh! The treasure map is gorn!" shrieked Wicked Ed as he struggled back onto his peg leg. Without a moment's thought, Jack and Patch dived over the side and—

Splash! *Splash!*

They plunged into the heaving waves. As Jack swam after the precious map, Cap'n Hubbard and his crew were locked in a ferocious battle with Wicked Ed and his hairy gang. Within moments the huge seas had swept Jack and Patch far away from the *Goosey Gander.*

All seemed lost!

But luckily, just in the nick of time, Jack, Patch, and the treasure map were rescued by an Owl and a Pussycat sailing by in a beautiful pea-green boat.

A day later, they all landed on a beach where the Bong Tree grew. The Owl and the Pussycat were in search of the wood where the Piggy-wig stood. "It's just over there," said Jack, pointing out the way on the map. And he waved his friends good-bye.

Jack peered at the map again. "Look, Patch," he said. "The treasure lies far to the east, deep in the Dark, Dark Wood. We go this way." So they hurried off.

Head that way....

Jack and Patch had not gone far when they came to a cottage made of gingerbread and candy. By now they were hungry.

"Mmm! This is good," said Jack with a giggle, munching a large chunk of butterscotch. Once they were full of sweet treats, they scurried off again.

Which way now, Patch?

Along the winding path, Jack and Patch bumped into two small children. "Hello. Who are you?" asked Jack.

"I'm Hansel," said the little boy.

"And I'm Gretel," said the little girl. "We're lost and hungry and can't find our way home."

"Well," said Jack, "if you're hungry, you should go down the Hickety Pickety Path to Gingerbread Cottage. It's made of real gingerbread and covered in candy. Look, it's right here on my map. And just beyond the cottage is the Straight and Narrow Path, which will lead you safely home."

"Wow! Candy! Yippee!" shouted Hansel and Gretel, and off they ran.

Jack and Patch pressed on through the woods toward Banbury Cross.

Banbury Cross, here we come!

Yummy!

Scrummy!

Hansel and Gretel followed Jack's directions and soon arrived at Gingerbread Cottage, where they gobbled jelly beans, barley sugar, sticky toffee, and fudge.

CREA-A-K! The door of the cottage opened slowly, and an old woman peered out.

"Hello, sweetie pies," she cooed at the startled children. "You must be very hungry. Come inside and let me fatten you up with a nice hot meal."

Grasping Hansel and Gretel firmly, she pulled them into the cottage and bolted the door behind her.

She gave the children each a big glass of milk and lots of pancakes filled with sugar, apples, and nuts. Hansel and Gretel ate and ate until they had both eaten so much they could hardly move.

"I love children—the sweeter and fatter, the better. Heh, heh, heh!" sniggered the old woman.

She was really a *wicked witch*!

The witch grabbed Hansel tightly with her wicked fingers and locked him in a cage.

Then she turned to Gretel. "Hurry up, lazy bones! Fetch some water and cook a fine meal for your brother. I'm going to fatten him up for my supper. Mmmm—he'll be very tasty!" she said, drooling and licking her lips.

Poor Hansel and Gretel were very frightened, but there was nothing they could do—they were trapped!

Every hour the Wicked Witch fed Hansel more food, and every hour she shrieked, "Hansel, let me feel your finger to see how fat and chubby you are getting." But each time, clever Hansel pushed a chicken bone through the bars of the cage.

The Wicked Witch had very poor eyesight and thought Hansel was getting thin and bony. She became really angry — but then decided to eat him anyway. "You'll make a nice pot roast!" she cackled.

Poor Gretel was sent to collect firewood from the forest so that the witch could heat up the oven.

Fiddlesticks!

Hurry up, slow poke!

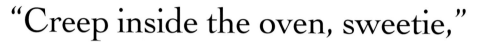

"Creep inside the oven, sweetie,"

cooed the Wicked Witch, "and see if it's hot enough."

But Gretel knew that if she did, the witch would

shut her in the oven and roast her for dinner too!

"I can't get in," she whimpered.

"You silly goose," hissed the Wicked Witch. "Look, this is how

you do it." And she stuck her head into the big black oven.

Quick as a flash, brave Gretel shoved the witch inside.

"In you go!" she yelled.

With a mighty *CLANG!* the heavy iron door slammed shut,

and Gretel fastened the bolt.

"Let me out!" screeched the Wicked Witch. "I'll be good!"

But Gretel knew better.

Quickly she rescued Hansel from the cage and they escaped

into the woods. They soon found the path

they had seen on Jack's map,

and ran all the way home.

Meo-o-o-w-w-w!

Meanwhile, on their journey to find the treasure, Jack and Patch saw many a sight. They crept past Baby Bunting at Rock-a-Bye Bower . . .

they found Little Boy Blue under a haystack, fast asleep . . . and they met a crooked man by a crooked stile, who gave them a crooked smile. Jack and Patch hopped over the stile and began to climb up Rumplestiltskin Mountain.

Halfway up, they met the Three Billy Goats Gruff. "We're searching for Greener Pastures," said Big Billy, and together they all looked at Jack's map.

"Look! There's Greener Pastures, just beyond Troll's Bridge," exclaimed Middle Billy.

"I'm going that way too," said Jack, so off they all went down the mountain until they reached the bridge.

"You first," said Jack politely.

Little Billy Goat set off over the bridge first, his little hooves going *TRIP! TRAP! TRIP! TRAP!*

But under the bridge lived a Terrible Troll with a huge appetite for goat.

"Who's that trip-trapping over my bridge?" he roared when he popped out from underneath.

"It's only me, Little Billy Goat Gruff," whimpered Little Billy.

"I'm going to gobble you up!" bellowed the Terrible Troll.

"Oh, no! I'm much too small—I'm only a mouthful!" cried Little Billy. "But my brother is much bigger than me, and he'll be along in just a minute."

"Humph! OK, then, be off with you," growled the Troll.

So Little Billy trip-trapped safely over the bridge into the Greener Pastures on the other side.

OK, Kid!

He's bigger than me!

Next, Middle Billy set off over the bridge.

TRIP! TRAP! TRIP! TRAP!

Out popped the Troll.

"Who's that trip-trapping over my bridge?" he yelled.

"It's only me, Middle Billy Goat Gruff," bleated Middle Billy.

"I'm going to gobble you up!" roared the Troll.

"But I'm only a tiny bit bigger than my little brother. My big brother is really fat, and he will be along in a minute."

"Humph! OK, then, be off with you,"

snarled the Troll as his tummy rumbled.

"But I can't wait forever, because I am getting very hungry."

So Middle Billy trip-trapped safely over the bridge into the Greener Pastures.

Now it was time for Big Billy to set off over the bridge.

TRIP! TRAP! TRIP! TRAP!

Out popped the Troll.

"Who's that trip-trapping over my bridge?"

he shrieked. "You're giving me a headache!"

"It's only me, Big Billy Goat Gruff," huffed Big Billy.

"Then I'm going to gobble you up!" roared the

Terrible Troll.

"Oh, no, you're not!" snorted Big Billy. He lowered

his big horns, charged forward, and butted the Troll very, very hard.

BIFF! The Troll flew high into the air.

"AAAAAAAARGH!" he roared.

And with a mighty splash the Terrible Troll landed in the river

far below and was swept out to sea. Big Billy, Jack, and Patch all

trip-trapped safely over the bridge into the Greener Pastures

on the other side.

BIFF!

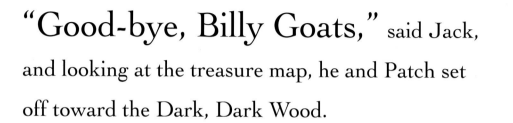

"Good-bye, Billy Goats," said Jack, and looking at the treasure map, he and Patch set off toward the Dark, Dark Wood.

At the end of the winding, twisting road, Jack met three little ghostesses, sitting on postesses, eating buttered toastesses.

"WOOOOO!" they wailed. "Beware of Dark, Dark Wooood!"

And then—*POOF*—they disappeared!

"Come on, Patch," called Jack.

"We're almost there!"

Wooooo!

In the Dark, Dark Wood, Jack followed a dark,

dark path. At the end of the dark, dark path, he saw a dark, dark tower.

Inside the dark, dark tower,

Jack climbed down

dark,

dark steps . . .

until he came to a dark, dark passage.

At the

end of the

dark, dark passage

was a dark, dark door.

Jack opened the

dark, dark door . . .

CREA-A-A-K!

Beyond the

dark, dark door

was a dark, dark

dungeon . . .

and within the

dark, dark dungeon

was a dark,

dark chest.

Jack unlocked the

dark, dark chest.

CLICK-CLICK!

And inside the

dark, dark chest

they found . . .

TREASURE!

And so, at the end of this **dark, dark tale,**

they all lived happily ever after!

So what happened to Cap'n Hubbard and Wicked Ed?
Well, that's another fairytale.